FUSION

GET OUTDOORS

Go Geocaching!

by Meghan Gottschall

BEARPORT PUBLISHING

Minneapolis, Minnesota

President: Jen Jenson
Director of Product Development: Spencer Brinker
Senior Editor: Allison Juda
Designer: Colin O'Dea

Library of Congress Cataloging-in-Publication Data

Names: Gottschall, Meghan, author.
Title: Go geocaching! / by Meghan Gottschall.
Description: Fusion books. | Minneapolis, Minnesota : Bearport Publishing Company, 2022. | Series: Get outdoors | Includes bibliographical references and index.
Identifiers: LCCN 2021001070 (print) | LCCN 2021001071 (ebook) | ISBN 9781647479718 (library binding) | ISBN 9781647479787 (paperback) | ISBN 9781647479855 (ebook)
Subjects: LCSH: Geocaching (Game)--Juvenile literature.
Classification: LCC GV1202.G46 G67 2022 (print) | LCC GV1202.G46 (ebook) | DDC 796.5/8--dc23
LC record available at https://lccn.loc.gov/2021001070
LC ebook record available at https://lccn.loc.gov/2021001071

For more information, write to Bearport Publishing, 5357 Penn Avenue South, Minneapolis, MN 55419. Printed in the United States of America.

Image Credits

Cover, © N.MacTavish/Shutterstock, © jeff Metzger/Shutterstock, © Selin Aydogan/Shutterstock; 1M, © N.MacTavish/Shutterstock; 1BR, © Pavel K/Shutterstock; 1BL, © Clker-Free-Vector-Images/Pixabay; 4, © Pavel K/Shutterstock; 5, © SpeedKingz/Shutterstock; 6, © photocrazed_jls/Shutterstock; 7B, © Grobler du Preez/Shutterstock; 7T, © ra-photos/Getty Images; 8, © Pavel K/Shutterstock; 9, © Eureka_89/Getty Images; 10, © ra-photos/Getty Images; 11, © Geert Smet/Shutterstock; 12, © Andersen Ross Photography Inc/Getty Images; 13, © zlikovec/Getty Images; 15, © LARISA SHPINEVA/Getty Images; 16, © tirc83/Getty Images; 17L, © Brester Irina/Shutterstock; 17RB, © OpenClipart-Vectors/Pixabay; 17RT, © b0red/Pixabay; 18, © Jeff Willhelm/MCT/Newscom; 19, © Jennifer Babson/Newscom; 20, © maradek/Getty Images; 21, © XiXinXing/Shutterstock; 22, © CarmenMurillo/Getty Images; 23, © Noel Hendrickson/Getty Images; 23BR, © Pavel K/Shutterstock; Background, © Merggy/Shutterstock, © Clker-Free-Vector-Images/Pixabay, © Shirstok/Shutterstock; Design elements, © NotionPic/Shutterstock, © JungleOutThere/Shutterstock, © Colorlife/Shutterstock, © Janjf93/Pixabay, © aliaksei kruhlenia/Shutterstock, © Kaliene/Pixabay, © Sudowoodo/Shutterstock

CONTENTS

A GEOCACHING ADVENTURE

Do you ever imagine you're on a **treasure** hunt? You don't have to be a pirate to search high and low. Go geocaching!

Geocaching has been around for more than 20 years.

Geocaching is a fun activity where you look for things hidden outside. You can do it with your friends. Just make sure to bring an adult to help you along the way.

Geocaching is a great way to get outdoors.

ALL ABOUT CACHES

So what are you looking for? Hidden boxes called **caches**! People hide them outside where they can blend in. They might be covered with branches or leaves. They could be the same color as rocks or plants.

Cache sounds just like the word cash!

When you go outdoors, you can look for the boxes. It's like a game to play with people you have never met.

Caches can be big or small. They are always **waterproof** to protect what's inside.

GPS MARKS THE SPOT

Caches can be hidden anywhere outside. How will you know where to look? First, have an adult help you look at a geocaching website. Check to see if there are any caches hidden near you.

The word geocache has two parts. Geo means Earth. Cache means a hiding place.

Each cache has a special set of numbers called **coordinates.** When you put these numbers into a cell phone or another **device** that uses **GPS**, you will know where to go.

There are more than 3,000 caches in the United States!

HOW TO CHOOSE A CACHE

When you pick your cache, look at its **ratings**. There are two kinds of ratings, and each is scored out of five stars.

The **difficulty** (D) rating tells you how easy or hard it is to find the cache.

Terrain means land. A cache's terrain (T) rating tells you if the area is easy or hard to get to.

A rating of one is the easiest. Five is the hardest. Start with low D/T ratings.

EXPLORING

You've picked a cache with the perfect D/T rating. Now what? Let the GPS in your phone or device lead the way. It will get you about 30 feet (9 m) from a cache. Then, it's up to you to do the rest by exploring!

Be on the lookout for anything out of place. Look in tree branches or around walls. Look under bushes and rocks.

Make sure you wear the right clothes for the weather. Wear comfy shoes or hiking boots.

GEOCACHING AND NATURE

When you search for caches, be sure you don't step on plants or flowers. Give animals plenty of space, too. You will never have to harm nature to find a cache.

Caches are never buried. You won't have to do any digging during your treasure hunt.

Bird nests are often hidden, just like geocaches. But remember, caches will never be found in an animal's home.

WHAT'S INSIDE?

You found it! Now, open up the box to see what's inside. Every cache has a **logbook**. Add your name and the date to the book.

The other items in a cache are called SWAG. This stands for stuff we all get. There could be small toys or key chains. You can put your own small piece of SWAG in the cache and take another one with you.

The SWAG you leave in the cache should be worth the same as the item you take.

TRACKABLES

Some caches have things called trackables inside. These small items are moved from cache to cache. You can tell they are trackables because they have special **codes** on them.

You can take a trackable out of the cache. But you must put it in another cache. You should only take one if you are going geocaching again soon.

How can you find out where a trackable has been? Look up a trackable's code online. There, a list shows all the different places the trackable has traveled! Be sure to add your name and where you found it to the list.

Some trackables are called Travel Bugs.

FUN FOR ALL

What should you do when you're done? Put the cache back exactly how you found it. You don't want to make it harder or easier for the next geocacher to find.

You're not finished yet! Back home, have an adult help you go back onto the geocaching website. You can sign the online logbook and let everyone know you found the cache.

GEOCACHING ANYWHERE

You can go geocaching almost anywhere! Look for caches close to your home.

Caches can be found out in the wild or in big cities. Many **state parks** have geocaching, too. You'll have fun wherever you go.

I can't wait to see you again the next time we GET OUTDOORS!

GLOSSARY

caches hidden boxes with small items inside

codes sets of letters or symbols that give a message

coordinates sets of numbers used to find a point on a map

device a machine or tool that does a job

difficulty how hard something is to do

GPS a system that uses satellites to give location information

logbook a written record of activities or events

ratings measurements of a thing's features, especially when compared with other things of the same type

state parks areas of land set aside by state governments to protect the animals and plants that live there

terrain ground or land

treasure something valuable that is hidden or kept in a safe place

waterproof able to keep water from passing through

INDEX